This book is dedicated to *J.L.P.* (you know who you are)....

My something better.

ADaPt Publishing (brooklynsongz@yahoo.com)

Copyright 2006 Andrea Pitts
ISBN 978-0-6151-3675-2
Front cover illustrations remain the copyright of Trevor Pitts, 2006
The acknowledgements on the following page constitute an extention of this copyright page

ACKNOWLEDGEMENTS

First and foremost I would like to thank my heavenly Father Jehovah for giving me the wonderful gift of life. Each day I thank you for allowing me to serve you. I would like to thank Trevor Pitts for his artistic expertise on the cover of my book. Thank you to everyone who has in some way, shape, or form been an inspiration to me, some more than others. Thank you to my husband Jarreau for his support. If you hadn't kept the kids for me all those days I would have never finished this book. My children have been the driving forces behind everything I do because it is for them that I live. Thank you to my mom for just being who she is. That is enough for me. My sister Nikki, thank you for tediously reading through this material so I won't look crazy when people are reading my book. I love you for being my sister in the physical and spiritual sense of the word (7/24/04) and I thank you for being my friend. Thank you to my brothers for always looking out for me. To my in-laws, thank you for accepting me into your family and loving me as your own. Scott, what can I say besides thank you? We have always been close and that will never change. To Mrs. Crystal Senter-Brown and Miss Tiger, thank you for showing me that I didn't have to be afraid of doing this. You both motivated me to complete something that I've been trying to do for a long time. For those of you who choose to mistreat and disrespect your mates, "Something Better" is waiting for them so thank you as well. To all of the people who read this book, I hope you like it. This is only the beginning.

DESTINY

It seems like yesterday that I met Lance and it's been over eight years now. Time goes by so fast. I remember thinking that Lance and I would be together forever, but sometimes things change and better things come along. He promised me so many things that he never came through with. We had some good times, but that all changed when he started trying to be "The Player". He had always been that way and I don't know what made me think that I could change him. He was smooth though, and I guess those smooth lines are what swept me off my feet all those years ago.

Man, if Jaylen heard me rambling on about Lance he'd have a heart attack. By the way, Jaylen is my "something better" that has come along. He's such a sweetheart, but let me get back to reminiscing. I can remember the day Lance and I met, and of course he had a line for me. I knew he was the Player type, but there was something about him that I just couldn't resist. He looked at me with those pretty green eyes of his and said,

"Hey baby, what's up?"

Of course I couldn't help but to look back and speak, so I did.

"Hey, how are you doing Lance?"

You see Lance was the new guy in town and all the girls had their eyes on him. I wasn't about to let this opportunity pass me by, you know, making all of the other girls jealous. So Lance proceeded to drop his lines when he noticed I was interested, as he was probably sure I would be. We were standing a pretty good distance apart so he asked,

"Cutie, are you gonna come a little closer so I can talk to you for a minute?"

I moved a little closer, but for some reason I walked slower, sexier, like I wanted him to notice me more than he already had.

"That's better. Destiny, right?"

"What did you say?"

"I said you're name is Destiny, right? That name is about as sweet as your face, cutie."

I blushed. I was at a loss for words, which is really unusual for me. Destiny at a loss for words, yeah right! That doesn't happen, but it did, and I knew that meant I had to have him. And have him is what I did. It started out slow and we got to know each other, and I was in love with "The Player" before I knew it. There was a lot in store for Lance and me, a little more for him than he expected.

Our relationship was going really well; at least it started off that way. We did everything together in the beginning. He bought me roses just because; you know all the sweet stuff. My parents loved him, but for some reason my brothers saw right through him. Maybe it was just the fact that they didn't want their little sister having a boyfriend. No matter what they thought though, I wasn't giving him up.

DESTINY

Lance and I would be having our one-year anniversary soon and I couldn't wait to see what he had in store for me, being that he was the romantic type. Our anniversary came and what should have been one of the best times in our relationship was one of the worst times. That day he called me as he usually did, but as soon as we started to talk I could hear something funny in his voice.

"Happy anniversary sweetheart. How are you doing?"

"I'm fine Lance, what's up I can hardly hear you, is everything alright?"

"It's probably just the phone. I called you for a reason though. I know you're going to be upset, but I have to work all day and I won't be able to see you today."

"Lance, what are you talking about? I asked you a long time ago if you had the day off and you said yes. I can't believe this!"

I hung the phone up while Lance was in mid-sentence. I couldn't believe that he would do that to me. My boo Jaylen would never do anything like that, but then again that's what I thought about Lance too. About five minutes after I clicked the phone in his ear my phone rang and I knew it was going to be him because he always called me right back after he made me upset.

"What do you want Lance...?"

This is how I answered the phone when he'd done something wrong and I knew it was him on the line.

"... I'm really not in the mood to..."

I was cut off.

"Don't be calling me Lance."

"Oh, I'm sorry Nigel."

Nigel is my best friend, and when Lance and I got together they couldn't stand each other.

"What did he do to you now cause I will beat him down."

"I don't know why the two of you carry on like this, and y'all used to be boys. Anyway, it's not as bad as it sounds. He just told me he has to work all night and I'm disappointed about us not being together on our anniversary."

"Destiny, you know exactly why Lance and I aren't cool anymore, and it's because I know how he's going to try and dog you out and I don't want to see that happen to you. Well, since you're going to be in the house anyway do you want to go to the movies or something?"

"That sounds cool. Just come by to get me in about an hour. I'll be ready."

"OK Des, see you then."

"Nigel, thanks for caring, but things are fine between me and Lance. Bye."

We hung up the phone and I ran up the stairs to find something to wear. You know, I think the real reason Nigel can't stand Lance is because he's got a little thing for me like I had for him when he was with Melody. Nigel is a sweetheart, but things would have never worked out between us because we know absolutely too much about each other.

An hour later on the dot Mr. Punctual was ringing the doorbell, and I was still doing my hair. I ran downstairs to open the door for him and he was looking sharp as usual.

"You not ready yet slow poke?"

"Almost, just give me about five more minutes."

I was finally ready and just as I went to open the door and leave the phone rang. I wasn't going to answer it, but for some reason I thought that it was going to be Lance so I picked it up. Although I was mad at him, my voice smiled when I realized that it was him on the other end of the line. Nigel could tell that it was Lance on the phone and he started getting impatient. Lance and I talked for a few more minutes. He apologized about not being able to be with me, but I didn't dare tell him I was going to the movies with Nigel because he would have been upset. When we hung up I asked Nigel if he was ready to go and we left for the movies.

Whenever we went to the movies I always picked the flick, because I choose really good movies. Jaylen tells me that now. We were getting out of the car when I heard Nigel shout,

"I knew I was gonna have to beat this boy down!"

I had no idea who he was talking about since I had only heard him speak of Lance with that hostility in his voice. And that's exactly who he was shouting at, my boyfriend, who was supposed to be at work, standing there with his mouth wide open because he had been caught out there.

DESTINY

I couldn't believe my eyes; my boyfriend was standing right in front of me with another girl by his side on our anniversary. All I could do was cry and feel pain from deep inside where I loved him so much, and from where I thought he loved me. I think it hurt so much because it happened in front of the one person that had tried to warn me. But when I looked into Nigel's eyes I knew that he was only worried about me, not about the fact that he had told me Lance was no good from the beginning. I couldn't even open my mouth to speak. He had made me speechless once again.

Nigel grabbed my hand and pulled me close to give me a big hug. At that moment I felt closer to him than I ever had before. I felt protected and secure like my big brother had his arms wrapped around me. The funny thing was we never even looked back at Lance. Nigel wiped the tears from my eyes and we got into the car to go home.

I had never been more hurt in my life. The pain I felt was greater than any other pain because this was the man I loved, and he chose to hurt me on our special day. I was a strong person normally, but Lance always knew how to make me weak. It was like he had some type of control over me and even though the proof was right there in front of me, I still loved him, and I knew I always would.

When we pulled up to my house, Nigel offered to come in and talk, but I wanted to be alone.

"Des, you know if you need me you can just call me or come by, OK."

"I know, you're always there for me when I need you the most. I'll see you later."

"Love ya."

I walked into the house slowly, and it seemed like everyone there knew I had just been humiliated. I tried to be myself when I spoke to my family, but they knew something was up.

"Lance has called you about ten times in the last few minutes. What's up with that?" My sister said.

"Well, if he calls again tell him I'm not home!"

I stormed up the stairs and slammed my bedroom door closed. My sister was banging on the door, but I ignored it and I continued to let the rivers flow from my eyes.

NIGEL

I tried to tell Destiny about that punk Lance along time ago, but you know that saying "love is blind." I would never have told her "I told you so" because I care about her too much for that. I was sure Lance was ringing her phone off the hook thinking about how he played himself. I knew he would try and sweet-talk her, but I didn't want that to happen again. I hated seeing her hurt like that. The truth is, at the time I kind of had this crush on Destiny.

When we first met I was instantly attracted to her, and later I found out that she felt the same way. I had a girlfriend at the time, but I gave Destiny my number anyway. She didn't call me until about two weeks later, but I was happy to hear her voice. I think we both wanted more in the beginning, but the more we got to know each other the more we realized that we should just be friends - best friends. There were some periods of time when we snuck in a little kiss here and there or maybe even a little more, but I never overstepped the boundaries of our friendship because she was the closest person to me and I didn't want to mess that up.

After everything happened I called her to see how she was doing. I figured she probably wasn't in the mood to talk, but I called her anyway.

"Hi Mrs. Tillman, is Destiny around?"

> *"Yeah, she's here. She's been pretty down about what happened, but I'm sure she'll be happy to hear from you. That Lance has been calling here*

every five minutes and he done got on my last nerve. Hold on a minute, I'll get her for you. Destiny, baby the phone's for you, it's Nigel."

"Got it Ma."

"Nice talking to you Mrs. Tillman."

"Always nice to hear from you Nigel."

Her mother hung up the phone and for some reason I couldn't think of the right words to say to her. Maybe it was because deep down inside I really wanted Lance to get caught, but I never wanted her to get hurt. We could have been great together if we had met at the right time, but things never happen like that.

"So, have you talked to that boy with his sorry..."

"Lance, I mean Nigel, I don't need that right now. I know you're happy about this whole situation, but I'm still hurting. It's taking everything for me not to pick up that phone and tell him I love him and I forgive him like I've done so many times before, but the proof is in the pudding and I saw it with my very own eyes."

I didn't understand how such a strong person could let herself be controlled, but then again, love is a strong thing and I know she really loved him. I wished that I could fix all of her pain but I couldn't. It hurts so bad to see someone you love so much hurt so badly, but there was nothing I could do but be there for her.

"I'm sorry Des, I'm just upset. I can't help it. You know, if I didn't see all the pain in your eyes today I would have tried to kill him, but I knew that the most important thing was to be there for you."

"Thanks Nigel, for always being there for me; I love you for that. Someone's on my other line so I'm going to call you tomorrow because it's getting late."

"Alright then boo, I'll talk to you tomorrow."

Something wasn't right. I had a feeling that Lance was on the other line, and if he was he would try to sweet-talk her back in his arms. The scary part was, he probably would.

LANCE

I couldn't believe Destiny saw me. I had never been caught before. I didn't want to lose Destiny. I mean, I knew I was doing her wrong, but every player has one girl they keep to be wifey and Destiny was the one. If I ever settle down, Destiny would be the perfect girl to do it with. Don't get me wrong, I would still do my dirt, but she would be convinced that I wasn't, at least for a while.

Every time I called her someone else answered the phone and said she wasn't there or she didn't want to talk. I knew that if she answered the phone when I called she would talk to me, so I tried to call her one more time before I went to bed.

"Thank goodness it's you Destiny, I miss you so much I don't know what to do."

> *"You weren't missing me that much while you were with that chick at the movies were you?"*

"It's not what you think."

> *"Don't give me that what you saw is not what you really saw. I know what's going on and I saw it with my own eyes, so don't try to change things around now."*

"You're right, there is nothing I can say that will justify what I did, but can you just give me a chance to explain myself?"

I talked in that sweet and sexy voice that always made her melt and began to persuade her to sneak out and meet me so we could talk about things. I knew it would work because I know her too well, and she loved me too much to let go that easily. So I asked her a couple of times to meet me. At first she refused; she was strong like that. She didn't want to give in to temptation, but she did.

When I arrived at the park right across the street from her house, she was already sitting on the swing. I walked up to her and just stood there, and when our eyes met I knew she wasn't going anywhere. All the love was still in her heart for me so I knew she would come back.

"Sweetheart, I don't know what else to say besides the fact that I'm sorry I put you through this. I love you so much and I don't even know why I would think that anyone could ever compare to you because they can't. It was a stupid mistake and I apologize."

I knew I was smooth and that I had succeeded before she even said anything. Tears were running from her eyes and at that moment I think I realized that I really loved her and I was scared. I continued with my game because I definitely had to get her back now because for the first time I had real feelings for someone and I couldn't mess up now. So I walked up to her and wiped the tears from her eyes, then I grabbed her face so that I could kiss her lips. At first she tensed up and began to pull away, but when I rubbed my hand across her face she gave in and I kissed her like I never had before.

DESTINY

Of course, everyone thought I was stupid for taking him back, but I was so in love... so I thought. In a way I'm happy I did because all of Lance's doggish ways taught me not to make the same mistakes when looking for someone else. I think it worked too, because Jaylen has to be the best thing that's ever happened to me. I'll tell you all about him soon, believe me he's worth the wait; and if I hadn't been played by Lance I would have never gotten the chance to be as happy as I am now.

Well, after I got back with Lance, things were better than ever and I thought he had honestly changed, but like they say, you can't teach an old dog new tricks. I heard a new story about him every day but I just blew it off. I thought people just didn't want to see us happy. I was just too naïve to see through him. I don't know what he did to me, but somehow through all of the cheating and the lies I still loved him. I guess I wanted to learn the hard way, and that's exactly what I did.

We managed to stay together for another eight months before the bomb was dropped. My best friend Nigel called me one day and I was really happy to hear from him because we hadn't talked much since Lance and I had gotten back together.

"Destiny, how are you hon?"

"I'm all right."

"Des, I don't know how to say this besides to just come out with it. You know I don't usually get involved in your relationship, but I have to tell you something."

"What now? I can't believe you called me after all of this time to tell me something negative."

"Des, this is not about being negative it's about being a friend. Anyway, you know Jolandre, Lance's ex-girl; well she's eight months pregnant and it's his!"

"If one more person tells me that I'm going to die. For the hundred and twelfth time, it's not his! I'll talk to you later."

I was so sick of hearing things about Lance I didn't know what to do. Deep down inside part of me thought it was true, especially since Nigel had called and said something about it. I bet you'll never guess that it was true.

I know you want to know how I found out the truth, but it's a long story that's going to have to be made short. One morning I was getting ready for class and my doorbell rang. I figured it was Lance coming to pick me up but instead it was a girl. I opened up the door and realized that this pregnant girl was Jolandre. She asked if Lance had arrived yet and I said no. I invited her in because she looked really stressed. We sat down and she started to tell me the whole story about her and Lance. I was shocked, but I knew that it was the truth. As we both sat with tears coming from our eyes my doorbell rang again. I knew it was him, and the only reason I even acknowledged the fact that he was there was because I knew that he really loved me. I wanted to see him hurt worse than I ever had. He must have known she was there because when I opened the door I saw the tears of regret in his eyes, but I didn't let him say a word.

"I know that you're going to say that you're sorry and that you love me, but I can't let you hurt me anymore. This has been going on way too long and

can't do this to myself anymore. Lance, I do love you, but loving you hurts too much and I think we should just end this. So why don't you just leave and I'll try to forget about all the hurt that you have caused me."

One last tear rolled from his eyes and I knew he had felt the pain that he had been causing me for so long. I wiped the tear from his eye and closed the door.

That was the end of that chapter in my life, and it was time for me to turn over a new leaf. The healing process had to start somewhere and I was going to start it as soon as possible. I tried everything I could to keep my mind off of him, but I knew that it would take a while before he was totally off of my mind. I know I'll always have a place for him in my heart, but I knew I had to stop myself from wanting him so badly.

DESTINY

Although I had been nothing but rude to Nigel, I knew that he would always be there for me. I called him right after everything happened with Lance and Jolandre. We only talked for a few minutes before he offered to pick me up for class, and of course I accepted. When he arrived I was sitting on the front porch crying, but I quickly got up and wiped my face because I didn't want to put this all on Nigel's shoulder.

Before he could even get out of the car I had jumped up to go get in the front seat. Being the sweet best friend he had always been he asked me if I was all right. I kind of just blew off his question because I wasn't in the mood to talk about the whole situation right then.

> *"Nigel, is anyone at your house today?"*

"No, why?"

> *"Because I'm really not up for class today. You know how people are, and I'm sure half of the kids will know before we even get there."*

"That's cool, I won't really be missing any important classes."

When we got to Nigel's house I got nervous because I saw a car in his driveway.

> *"I thought you said no one was here."*

> *"And no one is here; my parents are out of town so nobody will be coming home."*

We went in and the first thing I did was run up the stairs to Nigel's room so I could lie in his big king-size bed. After a while, he came up too. Nigel turned on some music and sat down next to me and we began to talk. First I apologized for acting so shady after me and Lance had gotten back together, and he just told me to forget about it. Nigel was like the sweetest guy on the planet, and right then I couldn't figure out why I hadn't taken advantage of the opportunity when it came knocking on my door. Then I thought, whose shoulder would I have cried on if we had ended up together, and I was happy.

I looked over at Nigel and when I did our noses touched and all I could do is laugh. You see, when Nigel and I kissed for the first time that's exactly how it happened.

"'Member that Destiny, when you took the initiative and made the first move?"

"Don't even sit there and lie. All I did was push really close to you and when you turned around I was in your face like BAM!"

"I'm not lying, you made the first move as far as I'm concerned. For goodness sakes, you said…"

"I said, 'what would you do if I kissed you right now?'"

"OK then Des, what did I do that was so wrong?"

"You didn't do anything wrong Nigel, you did everything right."

Something came over me because I spontaneously grabbed Nigel's face and kissed him the way he had kissed me the first time we kissed. Nigel stopped me, but I didn't want him to because I needed to be comforted. But Nigel knew what was best for the both of us because what I needed now was something way past a physical thing. It was

something emotional, and Nigel had what it took to soothe my pain.

NIGEL

Although I had a thing for Des, first and foremost I'm her friend and I couldn't take advantage of her that way. I mean the only reason she wanted me was because she was hurt, and I didn't want it to happen that way. You see, Destiny had never gone all the way, and if that time ever comes between the two of us I want it to be special. She is very special to me and it breaks my heart to see her hurting like that, but I guess that's the way life is sometimes. I knew she'd get over it in time, and I'd be there when she needed a shoulder to cry on. It's amazing how much you can care about someone else.

DESTINY
ONE YEAR LATER

A year quickly passed after my breakup with Lance. Of course it was hard, but I did a lot better than I thought I would. It was really hard in the beginning because Lance called everyday and I had to be strong to resist. Everyone was there for me though, especially Nigel. I'm so glad that he is my best friend. I know now that all we'll ever be is friends 'cause he has a woman in his life. I was really happy for him though. Whenever I would talk to Nigel he'd say that he wanted me to start talking to guys, but I wasn't ready. I learned a lot from the whole situation and I just wanted to take my time. It was almost the end of the first semester of my senior year in college and I was looking at things totally different. I guess Nigel noticed we hadn't been talking much because he called me.

"Hello."

"Hey Des, how are you?"

"I'm good Nigel, I've been trying to call you."

"So, you've noticed that my lady has been taking a lot of my time. She's been kind of trippin', but I got her back in line."

"Trippin' 'bout what?"

"Oh nothing, she was saying that she's not comfortable with me having a female for my best friend, but I let her know quick that you were here first and I'm not giving up my best friend for anybody."

"You better have gotten that Lisa in line."

"Enough about that, how has my best friend been doing; find you a new man yet?"

"No, Nigel, if you must ask. I am in no rush to find a man after all the mess I just went through, but I did meet this guy named Jaylen. He practically ran me over trying to get my number."

"Well did you give it to him? Have you talked to him yet?"

"We talked once. He seems real cool, but I let him know right off the back what I had been through and that I wasn't ready for anything more than friendship."

"Don't go getting a new best friend on me."

"I couldn't do that I already have the best friend in the world."

"Well, Des I just wanted to check on you. Let me know if anything happens with this new guy."

NIGEL

I hoped Lisa could get over Destiny and I being friends because I really liked her. She hadn't really been nagging me too much about it because Destiny and I hadn't been hanging out as much since I met Lisa. We continued to talk almost every day, but I thought it would just cause problems with Lisa if I didn't set some boundaries in our friendship. I just had to show her that she could trust me and that she had nothing to worry about.

She used to ask me all the time if it would be different if it were her with the best friend of the opposite sex. I would tell her I wouldn't care, but she didn't seem to believe that. I could understand her concern, but I wouldn't have been with her if I still had feelings for Destiny. We're just friends and it is going to stay that way.

LISA

Nigel kept saying I had nothing to worry about when it came to his friendship with Destiny and I really wanted to believe him. He made it more than clear that they were just friends and if I wanted to be with him I had to accept that. I never admitted this to anyone but the truth was, I knew that Nigel used to have a little crush on her, and when I met her she was beautiful and that intimidated me a little bit. Don't get me wrong, I wasn't jealous, I just really cared for Nigel and I wanted to be sure that nothing would interfere in our relationship.

I just had to trust him until he gave me a reason not to. I'd never want anyone telling me who my friends could be, male or female. I had to be honest, she seemed like a really nice person and I guess that if they wanted to be with each other they would have been a long time ago.

JAYLEN

When I first met Destiny I thought she was the most beautiful girl I'd ever seen. She called me once, shortly after we met, and she seemed very sweet. I just hoped that all of the things she'd been through didn't interfere with me getting to know her better. After we talked that first time I got up the nerve to give her a call.

As the phone rang beads of sweat formed over my brow, and then I heard her soft, sweet voice.

"Hello."

"Hello, may I please speak to Destiny?"

"This is her, and this must be Mr. Polite himself."

"Why you always talking about me?"

"I'm not talking about you, it's just that it's not everyday you meet a guy who shows a little respect, but I like it."

"I'm glad you do; so, when can I take you out?"

DESTINY

Well, I caved. I couldn't help but say yes to Jaylen when he asked me out. Things were perfect, which I hated. I wasn't ready to like someone else yet because I knew I wasn't over Lance. We continued seeing each other for the next couple of months, but I was letting myself get in the way of having something that I really deserved.

After a couple of months of talking to each other over the phone almost everyday and seeing each other a few times a week, I tried to cut things off because I was too afraid to let myself love anyone else. I knew that eventually our casual situation wouldn't be enough for him. I tried that whole "we'll just be friends," "it's not you it's me" thing, but Jaylen didn't want to hear it. I could tell he was hurt because he had worked hard to show that he really cared for me, and I couldn't give him a logical reason why I was giving up on something that felt so good.

JAYLEN

I was so confused, so hurt, I didn't even know what to feel. All I knew is I couldn't give up on Destiny. She was the most amazing thing that had ever happened to me, and I couldn't come to grips with the fact that she would allow one man to interrupt her life forever. She said we could be friends, but I couldn't seem to think of her that way. But I was patient and I didn't give up.

She didn't seem to understand that there were still men that could treat women with respect and not have an ulterior motive. For once I just wanted to love someone and not hear the words "you're just too nice." What does that mean anyway? Do I have to cheat on and mistreat a woman or disrespect her for her to think that I care; well I just couldn't do that. Somehow I had to show her that what I felt for her was real and that I would never do anything to hurt her. I knew it might take me some time, but I was willing to wait for the right woman, and the right woman was Destiny.

DESTINY

I knew that I didn't want to be with Lance anymore, but I knew it would take a while for me to be totally over him. At least it would take a while to get over what he had put me through. Everyone kept telling me that if I would just open my mind to other things then eventually my heart would open, but I was afraid to be hurt again.

Jaylen didn't deserve what I was putting him through because deep inside I felt that he was genuinely a good guy, but at the same time I thought I was setting myself up to get hurt. I called Nigel for some advice because I knew he'd know what to do.

"Hey Nigel, what's up with you? How are things with you and Lisa?"

"Things are going really well. I think she's the one Destiny. What would you say if I told you I was thinking about popping the question?"

"I would say I think that is wonderful. Lisa is the best thing that has ever happened to you and you deserve her, and she couldn't ask for a better man to have by her side."

"Thanks Destiny. Now, how about taking a dose of your own medicine?"

"What are you talking about?"

"Why can't you just let yourself be happy for once and give Jaylen a chance? I mean you said the dates were perfect and he was very respectful, so why end it before it even begins?"

"You know, I was actually calling you to talk to you about that. I mean, Jaylen is really nice and I feel kind of bad about giving him the run around. I have given him every excuse but the right one."

"Which is what, that you're afraid because you think you might fall in love with the right man? Destiny, don't let this one go, you deserve to be happy and that's what I want for you."

"Thank you Nigel, you always know what to say. I do miss spending time with Jaylen; maybe I should give him a call. I'll talk to you later."

JAYLEN

I racked my brain all day trying to figure out what I could do or say to get her to at least talk to me. Then I heard my phone ring. Lord knew I wished it were Destiny.

"Hello."

> *"Hey Jaylen, it's me Destiny."*

"Hi Destiny, how are you? I didn't think I would be hearing from you. You made it pretty clear that you weren't ready for a relationship and I thought being friends would be too hard."

> *"Well, there are a couple of things that I wanted to talk to you about if you're willing to listen."*

"Of course, in fact I was just thinking about you. I'm really glad that you called."

> *"Well the truth is, I only said the things I said to you because I'm afraid. I know now that I can't make you pay for what Lance did to me, it just wouldn't be fair. I know that I will never be happy if I hold on to what happened to me in the past."*

"Des, I know you've been through a lot, but I want you to give me a chance. Give yourself a chance."

> *"That's why I called, to tell you the truth and ask you for the chance to experience the real thing for once. I'm really afraid because I think I'm falling in love with you and I don't know if I'm ready to give a relationship my all."*

"Well when will you be ready, because I'm willing to wait for as long as it takes."

"That's just it, I'm tired of letting someone I say I don't love control my happiness. I don't want to make you wait."

"Well I'm not rushing you, but how about we get together and talk in person if that's alright with you?"

"I'm not busy now, so whenever you're free you can come by."

"I'm on my way. And Destiny, thank you for calling."

DESTINY

I'm so glad I decided to call him. It's funny, I remember being with Lance and trying to run around looking for something to wear or trying to fix my hair when I knew he was on his way. This time I wanted it to be real. I wanted to be myself; I wanted him to be himself. What is a relationship ever really based on if you put all the effort in in the beginning and then let yourself go when you get comfortable?

It had been about forty-five minutes since I talked to Jaylen and I heard the doorbell ring. I went to answer the door and there he was. When I looked at him I knew that I wanted to do everything right. I wanted to get to know everything about him and tell him everything about myself. I invited him in and introduced him to my family. He was the most respectful young man I had ever met. When I asked if he wanted to go somewhere and be alone so that we could talk he responded by saying, "No I'd rather just sit here and talk with your family."

With any other guy I would have been extremely nervous, but not with Jaylen. With Jaylen I was at ease. We sat and talked with my family for hours and they seemed to really like him. That was a plus for me because I'm a family person. Before it got too late we excused ourselves so that we could talk alone for a while.
We walked out onto the patio and sat down.

> *"So Jaylen, why would you wait around as long as it took for a girl like me?"*

"Because when I met you I knew there was something different about you. Most girls are worried about what kind of car you drive or where you work, everything but who you are inside."

"I guess I just learned that none of those things are important if you aren't a good person."

"I just hope you are willing to let me show you who I am and how I can treat you."

"I am willing to give you the chance you deserve. This time it won't be dictated by how I think you might treat me based on how I've been treated in the past. But there is something we should talk about quickly before we try to make this work though."

"What's up?"

"I didn't mention it to you before because I hadn't decided to take this seriously so I didn't think it was relevant. The thing is, I plan to remain celibate until marriage, and I feel that you should know that before you decide to turn our friendship into a relationship."

"Wow, that's the last thing I expected you to tell me, but I'm glad you did. I'm not going to pretend that it will be the easiest thing to handle but, this is not about sex."

"I know you have your needs and all I can ask is that you're honest with me if it is too much for you to deal with. I'll do all I can to make you happy, but I won't change my mind about that."

"It's cool, and it's nice to meet someone with values; and believe me I will show you on every opportunity I get that I appreciate you for you and not for what you can do for me physically."

"Thank you so much for coming by and talking to me. I'm glad I didn't wait too long to call you back. Well, it's getting kind of late and I have class in the morning."

"You're right, and I have to go to work in the morning. I just wish the night didn't have to end. Can I see you tomorrow?"

"Of course. You have a good night."

"You too, sweetheart."

Just that quick I knew this was going to be different. I didn't have any expectations; I just knew I wanted this to work.

JAYLEN

I knew then that Destiny was the one. I took my time and did things right because when I asked her to marry me I wanted her to know that if she said yes it would be the right answer. I wanted to do something really special for her on our first official date as a couple. I wasn't trying to impress her; I just wanted her to enjoy herself.

She loves seafood so I planned a big dinner at The Majestic, the biggest, fanciest seafood restaurant in Atlanta. Afterward I took her to this really cool spot downtown. It has a live band, spoken word artists, and singers. It's a nice place to sit back, talk, and enjoy the entertainment. It's also a nice place to sing a song to a girl that you really care about.

I knew she'd be a little surprised 'cause in the first couple of months when we were only seeing each other here and there, I never told her I could sing. She knew that I worked with some major record labels, but what she didn't know was that after all the years of writing and producing songs for other people I was getting a shot at doing my own project. It was something I had wanted to do for a long time, but I was worried about how it would come out so I didn't want to tell her. I hoped she would have a good time.

DESTINY

I had to call Nigel and let him know the good news.

"Hey Nigel, are you busy?"

"Never too busy for you."

"I know it's late, but I just wanted to let you know that I took your advice. I called Jaylen and apologized and I even told him I was ready to be more than friends. He came over and we're going out tomorrow."

"It's about time you start taking my advice. Have I ever steered you wrong before?"

"No, you haven't. Thanks for always being there. I'll talk to you soon. Tell Lisa I said hello."

"Thank you for letting me be there. Make sure you let me know how things go tomorrow."

I didn't get any sleep that night. I was too excited, but I had to try 'cause I had classes the next morning and I couldn't afford not to be alert. Graduation was coming up soon and I wanted to finish at the head of the class.

NIGEL

I was so happy for Des. She really deserved to be happy, especially after everything she had been through. Destiny told me she would be happy for me if I asked Lisa to marry me and I am thinking very seriously about it. I used to think that Destiny and I would make the perfect couple, but now I know no one could ever make me as happy as Lisa makes me.

Besides, if Destiny and I were a couple, who would have given me all the advice I needed? She has always been there when I needed to know the right words to say or the right present to buy. She told me what girls to bring home to mama and which ones to beat off with a ten foot pole. Her advice always steered me in the right direction; that's how I knew asking Lisa to marry me would be the right thing to do, but I had to ask Destiny for her advice on the best way to surprise Lisa.

JAYLEN

The big day had arrived and I couldn't wait to see Destiny. I called her when I got off of work just to hear that sweet voice. I told her I'd be there to pick her up around 6:30 p.m. for dinner. She kept asking where we were going but I decided to keep it a secret. All I told her was that she should dress nice.

It was 6:15 p.m. and I was on my way to pick her up. I stopped and picked up some flowers for her. I was so anxious to see her face when I arrived. I pulled up right on time. I got out and walked to her door and Destiny's father opened the door. I shook his hand and he invited me in. Her sister Keisha went upstairs to get Destiny for me. I stood and waited in anticipation. Would she think I was just trying to impress her with the flowers, the restaurant, and the singing? Maybe she would see it for what it really was, a token of my gratitude for every thing she was about to offer me.

I saw her as she began to walk down the stairs and she looked beautiful. I couldn't wait to see how she would enjoy everything. I thought I would have been a nervous wreck, but when someone makes you feel like Destiny makes me feel you can't be nervous. I just wanted to start the first day of what I hoped would be the rest of our lives off on the right track.

"So, are you ready?"

"Yes, I can't wait to see where we're going."

DESTINY

When he got there to pick me up he was looking so good. I hoped he thought the same about me. It was time for us to go, and my parents walked us to the door. Jaylen said,

"You look so beautiful tonight."

"Thanks Jaylen, you look really nice yourself. Thank you for the flowers they're beautiful."

We continued to talk and listen to music on the way to dinner. To my surprise we pulled up to one of the nicest restaurants in town.

"I can't believe it! We're eating at The Majestic. How did you pull that off? People have to make reservations weeks in advance to get in here."

"I knew that you loved seafood so I asked my boss to pull a few strings for me. I told him how important this night was for me, and he spoke to his good friend who owns the restaurant."

"Well thank you, I've always wanted to come here."

We ate dinner and enjoyed some really good conversation. I couldn't have asked for a better date. I thought the night was over but then he asked,

"Are you ready for a little bit of fun?"

"What could be better than what we just enjoyed?"

"I thought it would be nice to take you downtown to Clarion's."

"That's cool, what's going on tonight?"

"They have Expressions tonight; there are spoken word artists, singers, and a live band. I thought you might enjoy it."

"It sounds like a lot of fun, and I was hoping we could spend a little more time together."

JAYLEN

She seemed to really enjoy herself and I was delighted about that. As we got closer to Clarion's I got a little more apprehensive about the whole singing thing. I've been doing music for so long that it's become like second nature to me, but the idea of singing a song to Destiny made me feel like I was just starting out.

We pulled up to the club and I parked the car. I walked around to open her door and help her out of the car. As we walked in all eyes were on Destiny. She had to be the most attractive woman there. The thing I love about Destiny is that she's totally oblivious to the fact that she's gorgeous and when she's with me it's like no one else is around.

When we got inside the band "Genuine Harmony" was playing some old school jams. We sat down at the table and enjoyed the atmosphere.

"This really good spoken word artist is supposed to be performing tonight. I think you'll like her a lot."

"I love poetry. I used to write back when I was in high school. I don't know why I stopped."

"Do you still have any of your poems?"

"Yeah, I have a whole portfolio of poems and songs. Some of them are actually pretty good, but my Dad never thought I'd get anywhere with them. Instead of putting up a big

fight I just enrolled in school and majored in Business Management with a minor in Accounting."

"So if your Dad had been behind you do you think you would have pursued it?"

"Maybe one day I still can, but I'm glad that I went to school. It's good to have something to fall back on. Look at you, you made your way into the music Industry, but if that ever fell through you'd always have your Psychology degree to fall back on."

"I can't believe your only twenty-one. Most young ladies your age don't even know what they want out of life, but you know what you want and how you're going to get it."

"You're talking about me being mature. You're a twenty- five-year-old college graduate, working at a major record label. Not many men your age can say they've made those types of accomplishments. Sounds like you knew what you wanted and you got it."

"Oh, here comes Crystalline Jewel, the spoken word artist I told you about."

We sat back and listened to her poetry. Her pieces were so meaningful. I tried to pretend that I was paying close attention to Crystalline, but I couldn't get my mind off of my performance, which was coming up next. I must have looked nervous because Destiny asked,

"What's the matter, Jaylen?"

"Oh nothing, just listening to her speak. Are you having a good time?"

"Yes, I've never been to anything like this before."

The moment came when I had to excuse myself from the table so she wouldn't know that I was singing. I told her that I was going to the restroom, but instead I went backstage and waited to be announced.

DESTINY

Was I crazy to miss someone I'd spent the last three hours with? I wondered what was taking him so long because he was about to miss the next act. The MC for the night introduced the next act by telling a little bit about the guy.

"This next act has been on the grind at this music thing for quite a while. He thought he would come out and share a little something with us. He calls this one 'She Has Everything' and he dedicates it to the most ravishing woman in the room."

I thought to myself, "that is so sweet." If anyone ever did anything like that for me I don't know what I'd do.

I heard this smooth voice humming to the music. I couldn't quite see him yet because the stage was so dark. When the spotlight went on I was taken aback. It was Jaylen, standing there looking sexy and sounding sensual. I didn't even know he sang. He sat down at the keyboard and began to play. He kept his eyes on me the whole time. At first I could feel everyone's eyes turned towards me, but then everyone vanished. I could only see him, I could only hear him, and that's the way I liked it.

When he finished the song I was still in shock. He started to walk toward our table. He bent down and kissed my cheek and whispered in my ear,

"How did I do?"

"I can't believe you did that for me. I didn't even know you sang. Why didn't you ever tell me before?"

"Well there are a couple of things I didn't tell you."

"Oh yeah, like what?"

"I know you know where I work and what I do, but what you don't know is that my boss is giving me a shot at doing my own project."

"That's great! Have you started recording anything yet?"

"I'm still in the process. I have just about all the songs I need, but I need a couple more."

"I'm so happy for you. Congratulations! And Jaylen, thank you for the song. It was beautiful."

I knew the night was almost over and I didn't want it to be. I had a really nice time. On the way home I dreaded every second closer we got to my house. We pulled in the driveway and he walked me to the door. He kissed me on my cheek and said goodnight. I had never been on a date like that, and I couldn't wait to see him again.

NIGEL

It was 12:00 a.m. and I thought Destiny had to be home by then. I wanted to call her and find out how things went with Jaylen. I called her cell phone just in case her parents were asleep.

"Are you home yet?"

> *"You know I am, otherwise I wouldn't have answered my phone, matter of fact it wouldn't have even been on."*

"So you had a good time?"

> *"The best! He took me to The Majestic for dinner and then to Clarion's for this show called Expressions."*

"Oh yeah, I'm taking Lisa to Clarion's next Friday. I heard the band is tight."

> *"Let me tell you the best part, Nigel. The man sang to me, and you know that's as good as cooking for a sister."*

"You didn't tell me he could sing. He can sing, right?"

> *"Yes he can sing! I didn't tell you because I didn't know. He wanted to surprise me."*

"I'm glad you had a good time. Before you go to bed, can I talk to you about something?"

"Anything."

"I know I told you that I was thinking about asking Lisa to marry me, but I'm going to pick up her ring next Wednesday. I've decided to ask her next month on our anniversary. I need your help on a way to do it, something she'll always remember."

"Wow, that's great Nigel. Well, Lisa is really close to her parents, right?"

"Yes."

"Maybe you should do something where they can be there to see it. What if you tell her you're taking her out to eat at Legacy's where you guys met. Set an arrival time of, let's say 7:00 p.m. Then you could talk to her parents and anybody else that you all are really close to and tell them that you're having a surprise dinner for your anniversary. Let everyone that's invited know they have to be there at 6:30 p.m. sharp. When you guys get there she'll be surprised to see everybody but she still won't know that you're gonna propose."

"Dang, girl do you have a book on this stuff, you didn't even think twice."

"No, but every woman has thought up five thousand dream proposals. Does it sound good so far?"

"There's more?"

"Not really, but the best part is not only will Lisa be surprised everyone else will be too."

"Thank you, Destiny, but how am I gonna pull this off in six weeks?"

"Please, my cousin planned her entire wedding in less time than that. I got your back. Call me when you know everybody that you want to come, I'll call them for you."

I would have never thought of anything like that. Lisa is gonna be so happy. I can't wait.

JAYLEN

Things were going really well after our first official date. Destiny even invited me to an anniversary dinner for her best friend and his girlfriend. It must be a big deal because she's been helping him with invitations and reservations at the restaurant.

I was having a recording session at the studio and I invited Destiny. I had never had the chance to read any of her poems or songs so I told her to bring them with her. She said she would meet me there a little early so I could look at some of the material. She took such an interest in the things I was doing and I wanted to do the same for her.

She'd been getting prepared for finals and I was doing as much as I could to help her in that respect. Sometimes we read together, other times I quizzed her and sometimes I had to just give her space. Giving her space was hard sometimes, but I wanted to see her do well. She found out that she'd be graduating in the top ten percent of her class, and there were over seven hundred people graduating. I was really proud of her.

I saw her coming my way.

"Hey baby, how are you?"

"I'm good, happy to see you. I'm finally done helping Nigel with the plans for his surprise dinner. I think it's going to turn out great."

"That's good. Did you bring your portfolio with you?"

"Yeah. I'm kind of embarrassed to let you read it. I wrote this stuff like six years ago."

"You don't have to feel embarrassed with me. If it's good it doesn't matter how long ago you wrote it, and I'm sure it's good. Let's go up to the studio. I have about an hour before my session starts."

We went up and I started reading. Her stuff was amazing. After we had been up there for about half an hour I read this song called "All I Am" and it started with the words, "Why do you want me to be everything I'm not. Why can't you just accept me for the things I've got?" I continued to read and it got better and better as I went on. I asked her if she had a melody for it 'cause it was definitely a hot song.

She thought I was exaggerating when I told her how good it was. She said that she had an idea of what it should sound like and she started humming it for me. By this time I had about fifteen minutes before my session started. My boss walked in and I introduced him to Destiny. He asked me what I was working on and I told him that Destiny had written some songs a while back and I was really feeling one.

I asked Destiny if it would be all right for him to see it. She said she didn't mind. After my boss read the lyrics he agreed with me. He told Destiny how good the song was and asked her if she would be interested in placing it on my album. She couldn't believe her ears; this was something she had always wanted. She told him she'd have to sit down with him and go over the details, but if everything sounded legit it was a go.

Mr. Lafayette and Destiny set up an appointment to discuss things. Now it was time for me to begin my session. She said she'd stay for a while, but then she was going to meet her family at her Grandparents house. She wants me to meet her over there for a cookout after I'm done recording.

NIGEL

The night had arrived for me to propose. I was so worried about everything. I wanted everything to be perfect. Lisa had gone to get her hair done and I was on my way to pick up my suit. I invited about twenty people and everyone said they'd be there. If it weren't for Destiny I would have never pulled it off. I could never thank her enough.

My suit was perfect. My line up was fresh and I was ready to do it. I had no regrets because I knew she was the perfect person for me. I hoped she felt the same way. After I got home and got dressed I picked up Lisa at her house around 6:30 p.m. I could hardly wait to see her.

I pulled up to her house and went inside to get her. I noticed that no one was home, so I asked her where everybody was. She told me that her parents had gone to a jazz concert. I was happy to hear that they had left her in the dark. We walked out to the car and started on our way to the restaurant.

She said,

"Nigel, you know you didn't have to do anything special tonight. I would have been happy just spending some quiet time at home with you."

"I know but you deserve it, baby."

We pulled up to the restaurant and I frantically looked around to make sure no one was outside for her to see. When I saw that the coast was clear, we got out and walked in. I had reserved a special room for our party so no one would be in view when we walked in the restaurant. After I gave the hostess our names someone walked us to the room I had reserved. The employees had given our guests the heads up that we had arrived so they would be ready.

When we walked in everyone yelled surprise. The look on her face was worth it all. She was so excited. I was so busy looking at her that I didn't have time to see that Destiny had decorated the whole room for us. Everything was perfect.

Lisa leaned over and said,

"How did you manage to do all of this? Thank you so much."

"Destiny gave me the idea for the whole thing after I told her I wanted to do something special for you. She even called most of the guests and invited them for me."

"I know I had to get used to you guys being friends at first, but I'm really glad that you have her. I know now that she's not the type of woman to interfere in our relationship."

"Let's go sit down and get ready for dinner."

She was so happy about the party, and I couldn't wait to see her reaction to the proposal. As we waited for dinner to be served we mingled with everyone. I got a chance to introduce Lisa to Jaylen, and Lisa thanked Destiny for all of her help. The night was going just as planned.

We sat down to eat dinner. I planned on popping the question right before dessert was served. Now I was starting to get nervous, not because I wasn't sure; I just wanted the whole thing to be exquisite. All kinds of things were running through my mind.

What if she said no, what if I said the wrong thing? All I could do was pray that things would go right.

The staff came around to clear everyone's plates. Once that was done I stood up and told everyone in the room that I had a few words to say. I started by saying,

"I would like to thank our friends and family for coming out to share in this day with us. I'd also like to thank everyone for not telling Lisa."

Then I did it. I bent down on one knee and looked deep into Lisa's eyes. I said,

"No one could have ever done for me what you have done. With you I've turned from a boy to a man, and now I want to ask you to allow me to grow in to an old man right by your side. Will you marry me?"

Tears were rolling down her face. She could hardly gain her composure, but she did manage to say yes. We kissed, we cried, and we said our I love you's. Things couldn't have turned out any better than they did. Now I couldn't wait to start planning the wedding.

It was only a matter of time before our parents, followed by everyone else, rushed over to congratulate us. They were all very happy for us. Destiny came and gave Lisa and me a hug. She was so proud of me. We ate dessert and everyone went their separate ways. Lisa was still astonished by the whole thing. I did it!

LISA

I knew shortly after I began dating Nigel that I wanted to be his wife. I knew there were things I would have to get used to in order for us to get to that point, and I did. I am glad that I did everything necessary to make this possible, and I'm going to continue pleasing him so he won't ever get bored with me.

It's hard to believe that I almost lost him because I didn't want to accept his friendship with Destiny. It's a good thing I did because she was instrumental in his decision to propose and in helping with the plans for the party. I think I'll call her and thank her.

"Is this Destiny?"

"Yes, who is this?"

"It's me Lisa. I just called to let you know how much I appreciate your help with everything. I know I had my opinions of you at firs,t but I got over it, and I'm really glad that Nigel has you as a friend."

"You know I'd do anything for Nigel, and I understand how you felt at first. I'm just happy that you saw past it so that you could make my best friend happy."

"Thank you again Destiny."

"No problem."

DESTINY

Mr. Lafayette and I had our meeting last week. Everything sounded cool, so Jaylen will be using the song on his album. We agreed that I would receive points for each unit sold as well as royalties based on airplay. Even though I wouldn't see any money up front, it would eventually pay off, and even if it didn't, my song was being placed with a major label. There were a lot of other technicalities we had to take care of involving lawyers, executives, and lots of paperwork, but we finally squared everything away.

Jaylen had been working on the music for the song for the last few days. He said it sounded good. Things were working out well with his project. The song I wrote even had the potential to be a single. We would see in due time.

My graduation was a month away and I was so excited to start looking for a job. Jaylen said he'd give me the heads up on anyone who was hiring in my field. I got a couple of leads from one of my professors about two thriving companies downtown. I had my résumé in order, but I knew it would be hard to get a foot in the door when I was just starting out. I'm very persistent about what I want so I knew something would come my way.

JAYLEN

Destiny's graduation was the next day, and I'd been having a really hard time thinking of what to get her. A lot of people gave me money for my graduation, but I didn't think that was really appropriate for my girlfriend. Finally I decided. She said she had always wanted to go to Disney World but had never had the chance to go, so I had a travel agent plan us a five-day vacation in Orlando.

I wished I could have planned a longer getaway, but with everything I had to do, I needed to be back for work; and I knew Destiny would want to get started on her job search. It was a good way for us to get away from it all. She'd been working so hard in school, and I'd been working hard on the album, so we needed a break.

I finished up some recording while she was at her graduation rehearsal. I had to work really hard because the album was scheduled to be released in August. That meant I only had a little time to complete everything, including the plans for my record release party. I had a good team backing me up so I knew things would fall into place.

DESTINY

Graduation day had finally come. I could hardly believe it. It seemed like yesterday I was off to Kindergarten with pigtails in my hair. Now I'm all grown up. It was actually time to do things on my own. I knew my parents would always be there for me, but in some small way I felt independent.

My parents were so proud of me. I graduated Summa Cum Laude, with a 4.0 grade point average. If my parents instilled anything in their children it was that we should exceed any expectation that we had of ourselves. I never in a million years thought I'd do as well as I did, but hard work and the support of family and friends can bring you a long way.

My grandparents had planned a party for me right after the ceremony. I told them not to make a big fuss, but they invited everyone right down to my elementary school teachers. Maybe I'm exaggerating a bit, but they did invite a lot of people. The more people the more presents, better yet the more money. Let me stop. I had to get going so I wouldn't be late for the run through.

JAYLEN

The graduation was long like all the rest but we cheered like crazy when Destiny went up to receive her degree. I stood there with her family waiting to congratulate her, and then it was off to the party. It was really nice. I got to meet some of her family from out of town.

She walked toward us after the ceremony. I waited off to the side to give her family first dibs on hugs and kisses. To tell you the truth I waited because I knew once I had her in my arms I wasn't gonna want to let go. She walked up to me and I wrapped my arms around her and said congratulations. She squeezed tighter and thanked me for being there.

Destiny and I drove over to her grandparent's house together for the party. Everyone was there when we pulled up. They were barbecuing, listening to music, and playing spades. That was my kind of party.

After playing a few hands of spades and meeting most of her family we sat down to eat. We talked to Nigel and Lisa about how their wedding plans were coming. They had set a date for February of the next year. I hoped I'd still be around to accompany Destiny to the wedding.

Finally I got the chance to pull Destiny off to the side so that I could give her my gift. The tickets were enclosed inside of your typical "Job Well Done" card. When she first opened it she just disregarded the tickets and read the card. Once she was finished she looked at the two tickets in her hand and just stared at me. Next I handed her a bag with sunglasses, a bathing suit, and a beach towel along with all the brochures to describe the resort where we would be staying.

She couldn't believe it.

"Baby, I can't believe you did this for me."

> *"I wanted to give you something special, and you told me you always wanted to go to Disney World."*

"Wait until I tell everyone. What are we gonna do first?"

> *"I thought we would do a day of pampering when we first get to the resort. You can do anything you want - massages, manicures, pedicures, facials; you name it they've got it."*

"What parks are we going to?"

> *"We're gonna start off at Universal Studios and Islands of Adventure the first day. Later that night we'll head back to the resort for a romantic dinner on the beach. The rest you'll have to wait for. I hope you like it."*

"Thank you, Jay. I love you. I mean..."

> *"You mean you love me. I love you too. I have since the first day we met. Let's get back to the party."*

We kissed and she grabbed my hand and led us back to the party. Nigel was the first person she told. Everyone else followed.

DESTINY

When we arrived in Florida we went to the resort. Everything was beautiful. I was happy to be there with Jaylen. He's so special. I never thought I'd feel like that about anyone else and I definitely didn't think anyone could ever love me the way he does.

Once we got settled into our room he took me down to the spa for a full day of relaxation. First we both got full body massages. Then I got a facial, a pedicure, a manicure and a seaweed wrap. I felt like a queen because that was how I was being treated.

After a lot of talking we decided to walk to the bar to have a drink and get something to eat. We didn't want to stay out too late because we were going to get an early start at the parks the next day, and Jaylen said it would be a long day. I had never been down here before, so I didn't know what to expect; but I was looking forward to it all.

We got up early the next morning and had breakfast and then it was off to the parks. The first two we went to were like two parks in one, and we could go back and forth to each one all day with the tickets we had. Jaylen took me to Universal first to ride on a couple of things before it got too crowded. Then when it really started to heat up outside we went over to Islands of Adventure to get on some water rides. We kept up the back and forth between the two parks until we had pretty much rode everything. Eventually the night came to an end; at least it did at the park.

JAYLEN

Destiny really enjoyed herself, and so did I. The more I spent time with her, the more I understood why any man would be a fool to mess up a relationship with her. When she first told me that she was saving herself for marriage I thought I wouldn't be able to handle it, but when two people belong together, the physical aspect of it all is irrelevant. Don't get me wrong, I wanted her, but I knew when she told me, that it wasn't some gimmick she was throwing around just to make someone think she was a good girl.

Some people told me it was too soon for me to know that I wanted to spend the rest of my life with Destiny, but our trip sealed the deal. I thought it would be great to ask her at my record release party. That gave me two months to pick out the perfect ring, and get the preparations in order. I'll call Nigel when we get back. I need him to let me know exactly what kind of proposal Destiny will want.

NIGEL

The wedding was quickly approaching and the plans were coming along well. Jaylen agreed to sing at the wedding for Lisa and me and Lisa asked Destiny to be her Maid of Honor. We had picked our menu, our cake, and Lisa had picked out the bridesmaid dresses. Who knew there was so much to planning a wedding? Lisa still hadn't found her dress, but there was still plenty of time and I knew things would work out.

When Destiny and Jaylen got back from Florida he called me to let me know what a good time they had. I knew there had to be something else he wanted because we're cool and all, but we didn't usually converse on the telephone. Then he dropped it on me. He wanted me to find out just how Destiny wanted to be proposed to and he needed to know fast because he planned on doing it soon. It was easy for me to get that kind of information out of Destiny, especially since she had helped so much with my engagement and wedding plans. Fortunately she called to talk to me about the trip and I got the chance to ask her all of the right questions.

DESTINY

You know I had to call my boy Nigel to tell him all about Florida.

"Hey Nigel, what's up?"

"Nothing much girl, welcome back. So how was it?"

"It was great. I have to admit that I was a little nervous about the whole trip. I know Jaylen knows where I stand on the whole sex before marriage thing, but I thought maybe his patience was wearing thin, and he was just trying to get me down there and get some."

"You know he's not like that, and anyway, if he's waited this long why pay for a vacation just to get some when he could try right at home."

"I know, and that's why I went, not to mention he had already paid for everything. Nigel, I think he's the one. I just love being with him and talking to him. I never felt like this about Lance. He's never once pressured me to do anything I didn't want to and I never wonder whether he's out creeping with someone else just because he's not getting it from me. You know I actually used to blame myself for everything that happened between Lance and me. I thought that maybe if I had just slept with him he wouldn't have been with everybody else."

"The thing is you guys were young and you stuck to your values and he wasn't mature enough to do that. He probably never will be. Just be happy you found Jaylen and took my advice to keep seeing him. Now look at you talking about him being the one."

"Do you think it's too soon to feel that way?"

"No, Destiny, when you love somebody time isn't a factor. I mean, considering you really get to know the other person in whatever amount of time you've spent together. So, if he is the one, how would you want things to go if he feels the same way? I remember you told me you had thought up all kind of ways you wanted to be proposed to? How would you want Jaylen to propose?"

"I always wanted someone to do something really special, but now I just want the people I love the most to be there. I want it to be really traditional, you know, ask my parents permission and everything. With Jaylen I could care less if we were in a burger joint and he had a bubble gum machine ring; I just want to be with him."

"That's cool. I hope it happens for you, in fact, I know it will. I gotta let you go 'cause Lisa is beeping in on the other line. I'll talk to you later."

Nigel and I hadn't talked like that in months. He's such a good friend and I'm glad Lisa and I worked out our differences and that Jaylen is cool with my friendship with Nigel.

NIGEL

It was the night of Jaylen's record release party. Destiny was so excited with the song she wrote being his first single and all. I'm sure Jaylen had all kind of emotions going on because he was making the biggest step in his career and in his personal life. The party was at Phantasm, the biggest club and the hottest spot in Atlanta, so I knew it was gonna be off the chain. I rushed to get Lisa so we wouldn't be late.

As Lisa and I pulled up to the party we noticed that it was straight up celebrity style. I mean, I knew he worked for a major record label, but I didn't know it was gonna be like this. There was a red carpet, stretch Navigators, Hummers, Escalades, and paparazzi, and celebrities were everywhere. We got there just in time to see Jaylen and Destiny's entrance. They pulled up in a Bentley, rented of course, but it was still a Bentley. They stepped out looking like the hottest new celebrity couple.

We walked inside and got right to partying. His opening acts were about to go on. He had a couple of upcoming artists to get the crowd going before he came out. Of course the crowd got more than just a performance that night. Nonetheless, it was everything Destiny wanted.

JAYLEN

Everything was going well. Destiny looked beautiful, and our family and friends were there. It couldn't have been more perfect. A few weeks after we came back from vacation I found her ring. I bought a beautiful two and a half karat marquis cut diamond set in white gold. I prayed she would like it.

After purchasing the ring I thought it was time to speak with her parents. I knew she had an interview that Wednesday, so I went to her house and explained my intentions to her parents and they were overjoyed. I told them my plan of asking her at my record release party and told them I needed them to be there. I think the thought of asking them made me more nervous than I was to ask her because I wasn't sure what their reaction was going to be.

It was about time for me to head to the stage for my performance. I performed a few songs off of the album and ended with the single that Destiny had written. Now it was time for me to say a few words. You know, thank the audience for coming, tell them to buy the CD, and call Mr. and Mrs. Tillman to the stage. First I called Destiny up and introduced her to the audience and explained that she was responsible for that wonderful song they had just heard.

Then it was time.

"I'd like to ask some special people to the stage. First, my parents, who I want to thank for their love and support, and second, Mr. and Mrs. Tillman; would you please come to the stage as well? First I'd like to thank you for allowing me to be a part of your

beautiful daughter's life and now I'd like to ask if I could have the privilege of being a
part of your family."

I then turned and looked into Destiny's eyes and told her how wonderful the time with her has been. She started to cry before I even got down on one knee.

> *"Destiny, I've waited a lifetime to meet Mrs. Jaylen Moore and with each day that*
> *passes I am honored to wake up as your man; and now, as I stand before you, I*
> *know how much I want to wake up as your husband. Destiny, will you marry*
> *me?"*

Her tears wouldn't stop rolling and my eyes even welled up a little. She smiled and said yes, and with that she made me the happiest man in the world.

DESTINY

As happy as I was, I was more in shock than anything else. There I was thinking that I was crazy for feeling so strongly for him so soon and he was feeling the same way. I couldn't believe I was going to be his wife. I just wanted to give him a portion of the happiness that he was giving to me.

I didn't even know where to begin with the plans, especially since we were still preparing for Nigel and Lisa's wedding. I had to meet Lisa at the bridal shop so that she could look for her dress. She was so stressed about not finding one, but I kept telling her she had plenty of time to get the perfect dress. I saw everything that they were going through to plan their wedding and I felt so overwhelmed. I had to take it one day at a time and hope everything would come out perfectly.

I hurried to meet Lisa at the store because she would have killed me if I didn't show up. When I pulled into the parking lot of the store I saw Lisa standing there waiting for me.

"Hey Lisa, are you ready to find your dress?"

"I hope I find it today. Nigel keeps telling me to stop worrying so much, but this is going to be the biggest day of my life and I want everything to be on point."

"I know what you mean girl. It's a lot to do with just coming up with the date and figuring out who to invite. I'm trying not to think about all the work Jaylen and I have ahead in planning our wedding."

We continued our conversation as we shopped, and after about an hour in the store she found the dress she wanted and she looked absolutely radiant in it. It was a satin dress, white of course, with a halter neckline and intricate beading. Nigel will love it!

JAYLEN

Things with Destiny were going great. It had been three months since I proposed, and I loved her more every day. She landed a fantastic job as a Department Manager at LBJ Accounting, and my record sales were going well. All I could do was wait and see if things would continue to fall into place with the wedding plans.

We decided that we didn't want too long of an engagement, but we wanted enough time to make the proper preparations. We also wanted to let a little time pass between our wedding and Nigel and Lisa's wedding, so we finally agreed on May 21st as our wedding date. I knew those six months would fly by and I couldn't wait.

Destiny called me from work just to hear my voice.

"Hey sweetheart, are you working hard?"

"You know I am Jay, what about you?"

"I just finished going over some numbers with Mr. Lafayette about the record sales and everything is going as planned."

"Leave the numbers up to me. No sir, I'm just kidding. I just wanted to hear your voice before I went back to my desk. I love you."

"I love you, too. I'll see you later."

"Alright, bye."

We lingered on the phone for a few minutes because we didn't want to hang up. I felt like she was my first crush. After talking to Destiny I made plans to take her somewhere special. We had both been really busy and even though I tried not to miss a day of seeing her, I hadn't had a chance to take her somewhere and really enjoy her.

I took her to grab a bite to eat at The Garden of Eating. Destiny loves that restaurant. It's probably because the atmosphere is really romantic. They have waterfalls and full wall fish tanks filled with all types of exotic fish. I think the best feature is the table in the middle of the restaurant, which is off limits. It has a big tree right through the center of it. They call it The Tree of the Knowledge of Good and Bad. The rest of the restaurant kind of reminds me of a rain forest, and they serve really good food.

DESTINY

I was so glad Jaylen and I had the chance to go out together. I had a really good time and we didn't even talk about the wedding plans. I just needed a night to be with him and forget about everything else. I knew we had a lot to do in a little time, but I knew it would all get done.

After dinner we just went for a walk downtown and talked for hours. I realized everything there was to look forward to because I could learn about him for the rest of my life, and I couldn't wait to share more with him. They say you never know a person until you live with him, so I knew there was more in store for us.

We had finalized our guest list and got it down to two hundred guests. We had even booked the museum for our wedding and the banquet facility for the reception. There was still a lot to do, but I was focused on helping my best friend get through his big day. That was enough stress in itself, being the Maid of Honor and all. At least I knew my colors and who would be in the wedding party, and I even had a friend of mine from college, Beau Monde, who would make all of the dresses.

NIGEL

I couldn't believe the wedding was only two weeks away. I knew Lisa would make a beautiful bride and I couldn't wait to spend the rest of my life with her. She was so excited about everything and I was happy that she was able to have all that she wanted on the most meaningful day of our lives. We decided that we wouldn't waste any time trying to start our family because we both want children.

We had been together for almost two years and had enjoyed a lot of special things together, and we were ready to take it to the next level. Not that marriage isn't a whole other level in itself. There was no guarantee that she would get pregnant right away, so we did plan on enjoying some time together as husband and wife, but it's always fun to try. We weren't sure how many children we wanted at the time, but we knew we wanted at least two. I was an only child and although my parents spoiled me, I never had anybody to play with, and I didn't want our children to grow up that way.

Who would have ever thought that Destiny and I would have gotten married in the same year? I had known her for almost eight years at the time of my wedding, and through it all we were right there for each other. I was happy to have a friend to give me advice on my relationship, and she even helped me to plan my engagement and my wedding. It made me just as happy to be there for her too. We had both reached new plateaus in our lives, but it didn't change how much we love and appreciate each other as friends.

What would I have done if she and Lisa had never worked out their differences or if Jaylen and I couldn't get along? I guess if that happend neither of us would've been getting ready to get married. I know that probably sounds harsh, but I knew that any girl I was going to be with had to accept my friendship with Destiny. We always promised not to let our relationships interfere with our loyalty to each other. Don't get me wrong, we will always maintain a certain level of respect for each other's mates, but we are friends and we aren't going to let anyone take that away. A good friend is one in a million.

JAYLEN

The time was flying by. It was the night of Lisa and Nigel's wedding rehearsal. I had to head over to the wedding chapel around 4:00 p.m. Their big day was the next afternoon. Destiny and I had been a nervous wreck thinking about everything that was left to do in the three months until our wedding. We were burning the candle on both ends. Helping with Nigel's wedding and planning for our wedding had been keeping Destiny really busy.

She was more than glad to help with Nigel and Lisa's wedding, but I'm sure part of her would be glad when it was all over. It would give her more time to focus on our wedding, which was quickly approaching. But there wasn't as much to do as we thought. Beau had finished all of the dresses except Destiny's. Destiny had drawn out the design for all of them, from the Maid of Honor's right down to the flower girl's dress. Of course, she didn't let me see the design for her dress, but she did say Beau was doing a nice job on it and it would be ready soon.

I'm sure glad I'm a man. We have it so much easier when it comes to what we're wearing. I had a suit custom made by Beau, but nothing extraordinary, and my guys will just wear traditional tuxedos. The dresses are lavender in three different designs, one for the Maid of Honor, a different one for the three bridesmaids, and still another one for the flower girl. Beau had his work cut out for him with our wedding, but he was getting paid well for it.

LISA

Our wedding rehearsal went really well. Everything was just how I wanted it. At dinner Nigel and I presented our parents with gifts to show our appreciation for all they had done for us. I was so nervous because the wedding was only a couple of hours away, but I couldn't wait to be Mrs. Nigel Alexander.

My hair was done and I was about to have my make up put on. My mom wouldn't stop crying. The girls all looked beautiful in their periwinkle colored dresses. I had so many things going on in my mind and I just wanted to get through all of it. I couldn't wait to see Nigel.

It's funny how months of preparation can be over in a couple of hours. It was time to get the wedding started and I had butterflies in my stomach. The girls were walking down the aisle and in only minutes my father would give me away. Then I heard Jaylen begin to sing the song Destiny wrote for Nigel and me.

The doors opened and we began to walk toward Nigel and I couldn't hold back my tears. We finally got there and my father sat down. I was standing in front of Nigel and I was so nervous that you could see my veil shaking. The ceremony began and it was time to say our vows. Nigel's words made me feel so good that I couldn't stop crying. I even saw some tears roll down his cheek when I recited my vows to him. We said "I do" and we kissed. Just that quick it was over and we were husband and wife.

DESTINY

After being at Nigel's wedding I couldn't wait until Jaylen and I got married. The wedding party finished taking photos and we headed over to the banquet facility for the reception. I got a chance to spend some time with Jay once we got there.

The DJ was spinning when we arrived and those of us in the wedding party went to sit at the head table. Shortly thereafter, Nigel and Lisa walked in and were announced as Mr. and Mrs. Alexander. Jaylen came to the head table to talk to me until it was time for dinner to be served. After we ate and had cake it was party time.

The reception lasted for a while, but it had to come to an end at some point. The happy couple had a flight to catch in the morning. It was off to Jamaica for their honeymoon. I knew the two of them would have a good time there. Once the night was over I realized how quickly the day for me to walk down the aisle was approaching, and I could hardly wait.

NIGEL

The honeymoon was great and it was exactly what Lisa and I needed after the wedding. We stayed locked inside for the first couple of days though, if you know what I mean, but Lisa wouldn't let me keep her inside for the whole week. Our resort was right on the beach so we went everyday. Our tour guide took us to some really nice spots. We had a great time.

After the honeymoon it was back to reality, but I was alright with that because I get to spend everyday with the woman I love. We had moved most of Lisa's things in shortly before the wedding, so we just had to get things situated. She put her feminine touch into the house. She put knick-knacks here and there, decorative towels in the bathroom, and matching curtains in every room. It's all good, because this is our home, and I love the sound of that.

DESTINY

When I spoke to Lisa and Nigel and they said they really had a good time on their honeymoon. They both thanked me for all of my help and let me know that it was Jaylen's and my turn to sit back and let others help us. There wasn't much time until our wedding. I had been working extra hard at my job because I hadn't been working there quite a year and I was going to need to take time off for the honeymoon. Fortunately, my assistant is excellent at his job.

Jaylen and I bought a house, and I was living there by myself until we got married. Jaylen already had a buyer lined up for his condo. He was offered a decent amount for it. He would have to move out about a week before the wedding, so he agreed to stay with his parents until we were officially husband and wife.

I know a lot of people who thought I was crazy for continuing to hold out until marriage, and then there were the ones who didn't believe it was possible. The fact of the matter is, it isn't easy to make a decision like that and stick to it, particularly when you fall in love with someone. But, if more people would make those kinds of decisions, there wouldn't be half as many unwanted pregnancies and STD's as there are now.

It's not the easiest thing to ask somebody to be willing to wait nowadays. When I first told Jaylen about my decision to be celibate until marriage, I was sure that he'd think that I was crazy and say he had to move on. But I was pleasantly surprised when he was willing to try and he stuck it out. He has been honest with me the whole way through, but he never pressured me. He told me on occasion how much he wanted me, and the closer it got to the wedding he'd say he couldn't wait until our wedding night. That didn't offend me though because I knew how he felt and I couldn't wait either.

I just felt that waiting made it more special. Sex has been transformed into something so different. It's supposed to be something shared between not just two people that love each other, but between two people that have made a lifelong commitment before God and not just between themselves.

JAYLEN

There were three weeks to go until the wedding and everything seemed to be in order. Des was extremely happy with her dress and Beau did a nice job on my suit, as well. There are a total of ten people in our wedding party. It sounds kind of big, but there are some people you just can't chose between. Her sister Keisha was the Maid of Honor, my twin sisters Jazmyn and Jahnae were bridesmaids along with Nigel's wife Lisa and the flower girl was Jahnae's daughter Azariya. My groomsmen consisted of my brother J'Sean as the best man, her brothers Kari and DeVaughn, and Nigel. The ring bearer was my nephew Nadir.

We had three selections for our menu at the reception: baked stuffed chicken breast, lobster tail with shrimp scampi, and prime rib. After the wedding, instead of having the traditional rice thrown we would have 1,000 white butterflies released. About one hundred and seventy people RSVP'd, so it was going to be a pretty big event.

We agreed that our wedding shower would be a Jack and Jill instead of having individual bachelor and bachelorette parties. It saved us money, plus Destiny didn't have to worry about what kind of activities were going on at my party. Our wedding shower was two weeks before the wedding. It was nothing too fancy; our family members cooked and decorated my condo's community room. It was a nice time with our family and friends and Destiny got most of the stuff she registered for.

You know I had no say in what was going in the house even though she pretended I did. She always asked me if I liked this or that, but we both knew who had the final say. That was fine with me because my condo was a straight up bachelor's pad, not much style at all. She's free to do what she likes with our house.

DESTINY

The shower was at 4:00 p.m. and I only had about an hour to get ready. Of course my phone would ring while I was trying to do my hair.

"Hello."

"Hey Des, it's Nigel. Lisa told me to call you and find out if there were any last minute things you might need."

    "You know, I'm really not sure. Why don't you call Keisha on her cell, she's already there setting up and she would know."

"Alright, what's her number?"

    "It's 555-2406. I'll see you there because you know my last minute behind is just now getting ready."

At least I already had my clothes picked out, but I couldn't decide what to do with my hair. It was hot outside so I finally decided to wear it up in a bun. My phone rang again. I didn't want to be on CP time at my own wedding shower, but I had to get the phone because it was my baby calling.

    "Hey, baby."

"What are you doing, getting dressed?"

    "No, I'm doing my hair. Where are you?"

"I'm on my way upstairs to see you. I called so you wouldn't get scared when you heard me come in."

Even now I still get that queasy, I just fell in love feeling every time I hear his voice. Then I saw his face in the mirror. He was standing behind me and all I could think was how fortunate I was to have him.

"I knew you would still be getting ready."

> *"Stop talking about me."*

"I'm not talking about you. We both know you like to take your time so you can look good."

> *"Only for you. You better leave me alone so I can finish my hair and get dressed."*

I don't know why I said that because Jaylen came right up behind me and started tickling me. I screamed,

> *"Jay stop! I hate getting tickled."*

"I'm sorry. I'll let you get ready."

He gently kissed me on my neck and walked out of the bathroom, but not before he told me he loved me. I finally got my hair done and got my clothes on. We had about fifteen minutes to get to the shower and we were fashionably late thanks to me.

JAYLEN

We were only about ten minutes late, but that's early for a black affair. Most of the guests had arrived by the time we got there. About seventy-five people were invited and it looked like almost everyone had shown up. There was plenty of food and good music so I knew we'd enjoy ourselves.

Destiny and I thought it should be a casual affair because the wedding and reception were formal. Most people came in shorts and T-shirts, which was fine by us. I don't know about everybody else, but I saved my appetite for the shower because I knew the food was gonna be good. There was mac and cheese; fried, baked, and barbecued chicken; corn bread; green beans; black eyed peas and rice; candied yams; fried fish... man, there was so much food I got full just looking at it!

Everyone seemed to be having a good time. A few games were played and some prizes were given away. Then it was time to sit back listen to some music, get on the dance floor if that was your thing, or listen to marriage stories from the older family members. Since we were the soon to be married couple all the stories came our way.

They all had advice for us on how to stay happy for a long time. Some couples, like Destiny's grandparents, had been married for over fifty years. Some of them told us to keep God in our marriage, others told us to be good listeners. But what I liked the most was the advice to say I love you everyday and never go to bed angry. Whatever the advice was, we agreed to try and apply it in our marriage because we wanted to have a

long, happy marriage.

DESTINY

I was on my way to Beau's to meet the girls for our last fitting. The wedding was a week away so I wanted to be sure everyone's dress fit perfectly so that we could take the dresses home. My dress was going to my parent's house because I would be getting dressed there the morning of the wedding and I didn't want Jaylen to accidentally drop by and see it.

Everyone was there when I arrived. Kiesha and Lisa had already tried on their dresses and they said they loved them. Kiesha's gown was a lavender strapless dress that fit well at the top and flared out at the knee so she would be able to dance. Jazmyn and Jahnae were next to get fitted and their dresses fit well also. The bridesmaid's dresses were the same material and color, but had a halter top with a v-cut neckline and an open back. Little Azariya looked like a princess in her white and lavender flowered dress.

I was last to try on my dress. The only thing on my mind was that I didn't want anything to be wrong with the dress. I went into the dressing room and came out with a big smile on my face. I thanked Beau over and over again for the wonderful job he had done on our dresses. He made the dresses exactly how I wanted them. My dress was a Cinderella gown. It was strapless like Kiesha's dress except mine had a corset top. I had to wear a hoop skirt and a can-can slip to make the bottom of my dress poof way out. I was so happy. I thanked Beau again and paid him his final deposit before I went to do a couple of errands.

I had to head the mall to pick up Jaylen's and my shoes. I also wanted to pick up some things from the jeweler. While I was walking down the hall toward the shoe store I heard someone calling my name. I thought the voice sounded familiar so I turned around to see who it was. I couldn't believe my eyes. It was Lance standing there looking pitiful.

Part of me wanted to turn back around and keep walking, but the other part of me was curious to see what he had to say. I stood there in disbelief as he walked closer to me.

"Hey, Destiny, how have you been?"

"Fine."

"I know you probably hate me but I wanted you to know how sorry I was."

"To tell you the truth, I really could care less because I'm doing fine."

"Is that right? You gotta miss me just a little bit."

"I did for a little while, but my best friend helped me get past all of that and move on to something better."

"So you got a man now?"

"Yes, for the first time I have a real man in my life and next week he'll be my husband."

"Your husband. So you finally gave it up to somebody I see."

"You disrespect.... You know I'm not even going to let myself get all worked up over you. You've put me through enough and I'm happy now. You should move on with your life and take care of your child."

I suppose I offended him in some way because he started ranting and raving.

"Girl, please, I've been over you! The only reason I kept you around as long as I did was to see if I could get what you pretended not to want to give up. You'll never be as happy with him as you were with me."

I didn't even acknowledge anything else he said. I turned back around and kept going.

I finished up my errands and walked out to my car so that I could call Jaylen. When I got to my car someone had keyed the word B**ch in the hood of my car. I knew it was Lance and now I was really upset. I tried not to cry like I always did when I was upset, and I picked up my cell to call Jaylen.

"Baby, I need you to meet me up at the mall."

"Why do you sound like that? What's wrong?"

"Somebody keyed my car and I know who it was.'

"Who keyed your car?"

"I think it was Lance.'

"You saw him while you were at the mall?'

"Yeah. He called my name and to make a long story short he got upset and said some disrespectful things to me"

"I'm headed that way right now. Where are you parked?"

"I'm right outside of the main entrance where I always park."

"I'll be there in ten or fifteen minutes."

While I waited for Jay to show up I decided to go in and find out if there were cameras that surveyed the main parking area. After I explained what happened to my car the woman at customer service told me that the security office had access to all the video footage. I decided to just wait for Jaylen before I talked to anyone so that I could calm down a little bit.

As I was walking to the doors I knew there was going to be trouble. Jaylen had just pulled up and Lance's dumb behind was in the parking lot near my car. Jaylen had never seen Lance before because I didn't keep any pictures of him after we broke up. Before I could make it to the door Jaylen was on his way toward my car where Lance was standing, and I rushed out of the door and yelled,

"Baby, I'm over here!"

Both Jaylen's and Lance's heads turned toward me and then toward each other. As I walked over I heard Jay say,

"There's my fiancée right there."

When I walked up Lance had this smirk on his face as if he had gained some deranged type of satisfaction from vandalizing my car, and I just looked at him with disgust. Jaylen looked confused so he asked,

"Do you know each other from somewhere?"

> *"This is Lance, Jaylen, and I know he did this to my car."*

Lance jumped in and said,

"Prove it."

Jaylen hated sarcasm more than anything in the world, so he spoke up and said,

> *"Don't try to be funny. I'm going to try to stay as calm as possible in this situation, but I'm only going to ask you this once, did you or did you not key Destiny's car?"*

"If I did or didn't is between me and Destiny."

> *"Don't make me upset 'cause I'm not trying to bring this to blows, but I will if I have to. I'm trying to handle this like an adult."*

Lance always started talking in circles when any mention of fighting came up. I think he thought he was too pretty and didn't want to mess up his face.

"Listen man, I'm not trying to fight anyone. All I'm saying is she doesn't have any proof."

> *"I just have one last question to ask and I'm done here. Why were you over here by her car?'*

"Look, me and Destiny have a lot of unfinished business, and when I saw her car parked here I thought I'd wait for a while to see if she was coming out."

*"Just for future reference, any business that you had, and I stress had, with Destiny was finished when I put that ring on her finger. We **will** find out who did this to her car, and for your sake I hope it wasn't you."*

Jaylen grabbed my hand and we headed toward the mall. The video footage in the security office confirmed my suspicions. It was Lance that had keyed my car. We left our information with them so they could call us when they had a copy of the tape for us.

I dropped my car off at Jaylen's uncle's auto body shop and then I rode with Jaylen to the police station. There was silence all the way there. I didn't know if Jaylen was just upset about what happened or if he was thinking about the fact that I had seen Lance for the first time since our break up. Just as I was thinking that he said,

"So what did he say to you while you were in the mall?"

I explained the whole situation and he was kind of mad that I even acknowledged Lance when he called my name, but we talked things out and he got over it. That's the good thing about me and Jaylen's relationship; we always talk out our problems. He makes it easy for me to talk to him because I know that he will take the time to understand where I'm coming from. I guess that's why I knew I wanted to marry him.

JAYLEN

I was a little upset with Destiny when I found out that she had even entertained Lance in a conversation. After we talked for a while I understood where she was coming from, although I might have done things differently. She didn't mean any harm; I guess she just wanted him to know that he couldn't keep her down.

I dropped Destiny back at work after picking her up on her lunch break. She needed to file a lawsuit against Lance for the damages. We dropped her car at my uncle's shop right after everything happened and he got us an estimate right away. They assessed the damage at $1,693.42. My uncle agreed to hold off charging us until the case was settled.

I took the day off from the office so that I would be able to take Destiny to work and pick her up afterward. She was going to go pick up a rental so that she could have a way to work for the rest of the week. We both had a lot to do since the wedding was only five days away, so she wanted to have a car for the time being.

The rehearsal and appreciation dinner was two days before the wedding so I had to go pick up the gifts for all the people in our wedding party. I decided to get that done since I had the day off and needed to work the rest of the week. Besides working in the office, I had a show Tuesday and Wednesday, and I needed to get some practice time in for that as well. Everyone had been saying that I shouldn't work that week, but we were going on a two-week honeymoon to Paradise Island and I needed to get as much done

now as I could.

DESTINY

I didn't get my car back until after the honeymoon, but it was okay because I had a rental and then we were gone for two weeks. I couldn't believe how quickly everything was happening. It was already Thursday. I had a ton of work to do and I had to high tail it out of work at 4:00 p.m. on the dot to make it to rehearsal for five. My assistant Ishmael told me I'd have nothing to worry about while I was away. We had managed to get the most important accounts squared away so he wouldn't have any major accounts to deal with while I was out.

I ran into Lisa and she said Nigel was supposed to call me, but I hadn't heard from him. I had a few minutes so I called him.

"Hey Nigel, are you busy?"

"With all the litigious people in this world I'm always busy in this law firm."

> *"Well I was just checking in. I know we haven't talked since the weekend, but when I saw Lisa at the doctor's office she said you were going to call me this afternoon."*

"I never really got a chance to hear what else happened with Lance and Jaylen."

> *"Not much. They exchanged words, but you know what a punk Lance is. Jay was a little upset with me for even talking to him, but we talked, I apologized, and he forgave me."*

"That's good. I'm glad you're man can be civilized 'cause if that had of been me, you know what would have went down. If some cat tried to do that to Lisa it would be all over. Anyway, I didn't really want to talk to you for all of that."

"What did you want to talk about?"

"What doctor's office were you at when you ran into Lisa?"

"My gynecologist's office, why?"

"I just thought you might want to know that I'm gonna be a daddy."

"Congratulations, Nigel. Ya'll didn't waste no time. When is she due?"

"They said January 12th. I'm so excited, but Lisa's worried about not being able to fit into her dress on Saturday."

"Tell her not to worry. She can always go by Beau's if the dress feels a little snug, but I think she'll be fine."

"I'll see you tonight at rehearsal."

"Alright, bye."

I was so happy for the two of them. They said they wanted to start their family right away and that's just what they were doing. I couldn't wait to find out if it was going to be a little boy or a little girl. No matter what, I just wanted him or her to be healthy. Knowing Nigel he was probably ready for Lisa to quit her job and be a housewife as soon as they found out.

Jaylen and I planned to hold off on kids for a few years until we saved up enough money so that I could stay home for at least the first year. Jaylen would like if I stayed home until the kids started school, but I'm not sure about that. He wants four kids and I want two so we compromised and agreed on three.

I like the name Desylen (**_DES_**tiny and ja**_YLEN_**) for a girl and Jaydin (**_JAY_**len and **_D_**est**_IN_**y) for a boy. Hopefully we'll get one of each and then we'll just throw up a coin for the last baby. If it's a boy De'Kari (my brothers **_DE_**'vaughn and **_KARI_**) and if it's a girl Keijah (my sister and his sister **_KEI_**sha and **_JAH_**nae). Of course my mind will more than likely change before we have any children. You would think I'd want to stop the whole DJK theme our parents passed on, but I think it's kind of cute.

NIGEL

Lisa and I were so excited about the baby. I really didn't care if it was a boy or a girl, but I did want to find out when that time came so we could prepare the nursery. Lisa wanted to work right up to the end of the pregnancy so she would have more time at home with the baby once she had him or her. Fortunately, she had been working at the school for six years without taking much time off until our honeymoon, so she would get her twelve weeks of maternity leave as well as the eight weeks of vacation time she had saved up. Once I finished with my last few classes and passed the bar I would start saving money so she could just stay home with the next baby.

I called her before the rehearsal to see if she was home yet.

"Lisa, I was just checking to see if you were home. How are you feeling?"

"Tired, but besides that I'm fine. I'm getting ready for the rehearsal. Will you be here soon?"

"I'll be coming up the drive way in a few minutes."

When I got home there wasn't much time to get ready so I hopped in the shower real quick and got dressed and we were off to the museum for the rehearsal. On the ride there Lisa and I talked about how happy we were. She told me that she wanted to get started on another baby as soon as our first baby turned a year old. I was cool with that, but I wondered if she'd feel the same after going through labor.

JAYLEN

Destiny and I were pleased with how things went at the wedding rehearsal. I could hardly believe that in two days I would be married to Destiny. She made me feel so good. I couldn't wait to wake up next her every morning. Who am I fooling, I couldn't wait to lie down next to her every night. She's special and I'm happy that she let me love her.

We arrived at the dinner right on time. We wanted to have this dinner just to thank everyone for all of their help and support during the time of our wedding planning. After dinner we presented each person in our wedding party with gifts. Our parents also received gifts from us as well.

The ladies all received a Tiffany bracelet and the flower girl got a pair of diamond stud earrings. The fellas received gold pocket watches with their names engraved in them and the ring bearer got a brand new pair of Jordan's (call it crazy, but that's what he wanted.) Thank goodness my boss has friends in high places. I was able to get a really good price on the jewelry in exchange for some performances. Since Lisa's sister works for a cruise line we were able to get both of our parents tickets on a cruise to Tahiti.

Nobody could get over the gifts. Believe it or not, my nephew was the most excited, and he has every pair of Jordan's that has come out in his lifetime. After all of the excitement it was time to wrap things up. Destiny and I rode over together so I brought her back to the house and went to my parent's place. One more day and she would be Mrs. Jaylen Moore.

DESTINY

I stayed at my parent's house the night before the wedding so that my mom and my sister could help me get ready in the morning. My cousin Kayline came over at 9:00 a.m. to do my hair and make up. They say you need something old, new, borrowed and blue on your wedding day. My something old was the pearl necklace that my great grandmother gave to my grandmother when she got married. My grandmother passed on to my mom on her wedding day and now my mother is giving it to me. My something new were the diamond earrings that my father bought me especially for my wedding day. My something borrowed was the veil that Lisa wore at her wedding and my something blue was my grandfather's handkerchief to wipe my tears.

The wedding was starting at 1:00 p.m. I know they say all weddings start late, but I didn't want one of those ghetto two-hour late weddings. I wanted things to run smoothly. I was nervous enough without thinking about something going wrong. All the girls stayed the night at my parents too. The fellas stayed at our house. That way everyone was together and there wasn't a chance of anyone getting stuck in traffic.

I was on my way back to my parent's house to meet the girls. We all decided to have a girl's night out, but we didn't stay out too late because the next day was the wedding. I couldn't get my mind off of Jaylen. We had agreed not to see each other all day, but we had to at least talk on the phone. Just then my phone rang and I knew when I heard our song I knew it was my baby calling.

"Hello."

"Baby, I can't wait to see your face tomorrow."

"I was just thinking about you. What are you doing?"

"Laying in our bed thinking about when I can lay here next to you."

"I'm so happy that I met you, Jay." ·

"What are you doing?"

"I'm walking in my parent's house now. I just came from the store. Have you spoken to your sisters?"

"Yeah, I just hung up with Jahnae and she said they were on their way to my mom and dad's to drop off Azariya and Nadir. They said they'd be over to meet you right after that."

"Cool. What are you and the guys doing tonight? Nothing I wouldn't do, I hope."

"You don't have to worry about me. I'll be on my best behavior. We're just going to get a couple of drinks."

"Don't drink too much I want you guys alert at the wedding."

"I will be. The doorbell is ringing so I'll call you before we go out, alright."

"Alright. I love you."

"I love you too."

I sat there and waited for him to hang up the phone. I didn't want to stop talking to him yet, but I knew I had to.

NIGEL

It was the day for my best friend and her man to jump the broom. This was a good year for us both. I'm so happy that she found the one person in this world that is just for her and I found the same thing for myself. We have the perfect people to share our lives with and there couldn't be two closer friends than Destiny and me. I knew Lisa and I wanted children right away, but I had no idea it would happen as fast as it did, but we were very excited.

Jaylen couldn't stop talking about Des that night. He really loves her and something told me they were going to be very happy. They are made for each other.

JAYLEN

I was so nervous. The day I was waiting for had finally arrived. I hadn't heard Destiny's voice since the day before and it was driving me crazy. I just wanted to watch her walk down that aisle, looking beautiful. I knew I was going to cry when I first saw her. I knew Destiny would make me happy and I hoped to do the same thing for her.

We were going to be heading over to the museum soon for the ceremony. Everyone was just about ready. After we were all dressed we headed to my parents' house to pick up Nadir and Azariya. The last thing Des needed was to have to make a stop to pick someone up before the wedding 'cause she definitely would have been late. I'm not ragging on my baby, but she's slow getting ready to go to the store, never mind for her wedding day.

She could take as much time as she needed as long as she made her way to me. I'm happy I made it to this point in my life. Some of the guys I know thought it was a crazy move, especially since my album was doing so well. They thought I could have had as many women as I wanted, but I only wanted one woman and that was Destiny. She makes everyday worthwhile and I am glad that I'm spending my life with her.

DESTINY

I was running around like a chicken with its head cut off. My hair and makeup were done and my mom and sister were helping me get my dress on. It was really happening. I was about to walk down the aisle with the man of my dreams. I was about to cry before I even made it to the wedding. I would have been looking a hot mess with my makeup all running down my face and I couldn't have that.

It was about that time for us to get into the limousine and head to the museum. As we were driving, everybody was trying to keep me calm. I was calm in the sense that I knew I was making the right decision. I guess I was just anxious, so anxious that I couldn't think about anything else. All I could picture was Jaylen's face and hear those words "I do" coming from his mouth.

We had finally arrived and there were about twenty minutes until starting time. I sat in the back room praying that everything would go just right. My mom and dad were both walking me down the aisle. They are both very important to me and I didn't want it any other way.

Just as my nerves started to settle, my cousin walked in and said that they were ready to get things started. All the girls headed toward the corridor so that they could enter the gallery with their respective partners. I peeked through the door as each of the couples entered, and all at once everyone had disappeared. My parents signaled me to come out and I could hardly move. My heart was pounding, my hands were sweating, and my knees were shaking. I slowly headed toward my mom and dad and we waited for the cue of the music before the doors were opened.

The piano began to play and the doors opened up; and although the gallery was filled with people, all I could see was Jaylen. It didn't even feel as if I was walking down the aisle. It felt as if I was floating on a cloud. Jaylen and I looked into each other's eyes the whole time I walked down the aisle, and then all of a sudden I was there. My mother and father each kissed me on the cheek and walked to their seats.

Jaylen grabbed my hand and helped me up on to the platform. We turned and faced each other and the ceremony began. The time had come to say our vows to each other and I went first.

"Jaylen, when I met you I tried everything so that I wouldn't fall in love. We both know that I've been through some difficult times and at first I didn't know how to let that go. When I decided it was time that I gave love a chance, I promised you that it wouldn't be dictated by how I think you might treat me based on how I had been treated in the past. You accepted me with my limitations, and you've loved me unconditionally every step of the way. You are the very essence of love and I thank you for showing me, for the first time, what that really is."

A single tear fell from Jaylen's eye as he began to recite his vows.

"It's not everyday that we are fortunate enough to find the one person who was meant just for us. When I met you I found that person, and I knew that you were worth waiting for, no matter how long it took. I knew that although the cold weather had caused the rose in your heart to close, in time I could cause the sun to shine on you and allow your flower to blossom. With you I am more than I could ever be because...

He began singing the words to "She Has Everything", the song he sang on our first official date. My favorite words in the song are when he says,

"I never thought I could meet someone like her. Someone to make me smile after my heart's been torn and burned. But she's my pot of gold at the end of that rainbow, and she, she has everything."

By the time he finished singing I didn't have any makeup left, but I didn't care.

I don't think there was a dry eye in the place. We exchanged rings, said I do, and then it was that time. It was time for my husband to salute his bride. Most people tried to do that nice sweet kiss at their weddings, but not Jaylen and I. We went for it. He grabbed me and dipped me back and planted a kiss on me that made me want to skip the reception.

JAYLEN

After months of planning, it was all over that fast, but it was all worth it. Since the honeymoon, we've been enjoying ourselves as husband and wife. There's not much I can say about the honeymoon besides the fact that it was amazing. We got to see some things, but mostly we just explored each other. I mean after a year and a half of anticipation, there was a lot of exploring to do.

Things are going well with both of our jobs and Mr. Lafayette is even talking about recording another album with me. In the meantime I've been writing and producing for other artists, which is always cool. Destiny placed a couple of songs on an album with one of my label mates. Hopefully her album will do well.

I'm just glad Destiny is happy. In the past three months we've had disagreements but nothing we can't work out. I knew from the jump we had different personalities, but that's one of the things that makes me love her so much. I couldn't ask for anything more. We have the same interests, we support each other's goals, and our families get along. In fact, since the wedding, Jazmyn and De'vaughn have been kind of seeing each other. I'm happy to be the person who's turned Destiny's frown in to a smile. She's definitely changed my world.

DESTINY

Here it is three and a half years later, and I'm still as happy as the day I married him. Let me correct that - I'm happier than the day I married him because everyday we spend together he touches another part of my heart. We've been talking about getting started on our family, maybe next year.

Lisa and Nigel had a little girl. Her name is Nilisa and she just turned three. She's a sweetheart and smart as a whip. She calls Jaylen and me uncle and auntie. Lisa found out she was pregnant again about four months ago and they just found out they were going to have a boy. Nigel said they are done after that one, but we'll see.

Jaylen came into my life at the perfect time because if I had waited any longer I may have given up on thinking someone could be good to me. After all I had been through with Lance I had the mentality that every man would be the same. I knew that wasn't fair, but when someone hurts you the way Lance hurt me, you really don't care about anyone else but yourself.

Eight years ago I met Lance and he changed my life forever. He made it possible for me to find true love. All the hurt he put me through made me stronger. Now I don't have to deal with broken promises or wonder when someone prettier comes by if they will catch my man's eye. I know it's impossible, but if Lance could hear my thoughts I'd want him to know one thing. Thank you, because you paved the way for something better.